On Wing

Róbert

Gál

On Wing

translated by Mark Kanak

DALKEY ARCHIVE PRESS
Champaign / London / Dublin

Originally published in Slovak as *Krídlovanie*
by Petrus Publishers, 2006

Copyright ©2015 Róbert Gál
Translation copyright ©2015 Mark Kanak
Cover Photo by Viktor Kopasz
First Edition, 2015
All rights reserved

This book has received a subsidy from SLOLIA Committee,
the Centre for Information on Literature in Bratislava, Slovakia.
This book was partially funded by a grant by the Illinois Arts Council,
a state agency

www.dalkeyarchive.com
Cover: design and composition by Mikhail Iliatov
Printed on permanent/durable and acid-free paper

The magic of fiction lies in deluding
reason that it is fiction.

PART ONE

Curve-temptation

Since the world doesn't care at all about our intentions, it falls solely to us as individuals as to how we grapple with this reality, so that on the one hand it does not disconcert us and on the other hand does not encroach upon us. For only in this way may we arrive at the point to which we, through the influence of the imperfection (of possibilities) of this or that reality, simply haven't been able to internally attain for years or never have been in a position to do so. For where is it written, what the longed for actually is, without consideration of what its fictitious surrogate context is, in which we could embed it without actually losing it immediately once again. But these are completely concrete things about which one ought not to theorize lest we squander too much time. After all, who truly cares about the time that we are wasting away?

Life's necessity to expand forms and to find an internally ordered life in everything we encounter and that we experience, indeed in everything that is no internal order in itself . . .

The connection of the genetic to the frenetic?

⟐

A., my younger cousin who reads my texts, although I'm not too sure that he's reading them correctly. Again and again

I've advised him not to misconceive them as all too instruc-
tive, or, put another way, he shouldn't consider them as my
advice for his life. For me, these notes that always recorded
certain spiritual points of progression in flux and were always, above all, meant for myself alone—were a material, as
it were, that incessantly occupies my time because much is
encrypted within it (which, incidentally, *is a real pleasure* to
decipher). And whatever that which is encrypted may prove
to be, it would nevertheless ultimately be, even when deci-
phered, solely intended for me. It is for this reason that I
have in the meantime come to regard it as a waste of time
trying to explain anything to anyone, I regard it as a waste
of time clothing these irrational things in the elegant vest-
ments of rationality, which is fundamentally quite alien to
these things—serving only to strengthen the absurdity—
and perhaps the obscurity of it—all the more.

At the meeting today with L. and K., L. told me how he had
reacted some years earlier to a personal ad in *Mladý svět*. The
whole episode unfolded in a small town with a small main
square where she and he, the actors in this awkward situation, had travelled by bus for the aforementioned meeting
from other, even smaller places. They had met on that small
square, circling it for some time, side by side, keeping pace.
She was a young girl, a blonde, about twenty-one who had
already managed one divorce. L. asked her why she had decided to part from her husband. During the entire walk he

couldn't take his eyes off her shoes with the high cork soles and the colorful mini-skirt she was wearing. The girl simply didn't know how to answer the question, which only served to increase the already heightened tensions between the two, for L. didn't have any other questions to pose at the moment. "Was she at least pretty?" I ask. "No, she didn't seem pretty to me at all, actually." And so the two continued walking a while in silence, whereupon he suddenly said, "Ciao, I'll give you a call," and both quickly rushed to their bus stops and never saw each other again.

A Dream, May 10, 2005

Father and I—as well as an unidentified third party—found ourselves at a John Zorn concert on some island or other. It was part of a tour through several cities for which we had bought tickets to all the performances and to which we had traveled by plane to each of the different performance venues all over the globe. The concert was taking place in a huge hall filled with people. Smoking was permitted, which helped to evoke the unique atmosphere of a monstrous underground club in the midst of a complete wasteland. The concert is slowly about to begin, the musicians are already standing on the stage and playing. In retrospect it occurs to me that it must have been a trio on stage, and one of the musicians is a long-haired fellow who is turning grey, who reminded me of an ageing bard from one of those gradually dying out and yet unique examples of an elite that still

survive in small pockets from the beat generation. The concert lasted just a little while, about ten minutes, and for
me seemed, musically, like the 'ushering in' of the central
bard, John Zorn (who back then, unless I'm deceiving myself, had long hair as well), who until that point had only
experimented with his saxophone only by means of relatively modest—at least for his standards—screeching sounds,
which reminded one slightly (atmospherically) of the mod-
erately dissonantly swelling of a large avian orchestra à la
Olivier Messiaen. And even if only with a saxophone, for
the other instruments, most likely the bass guitar and the
drums, seemed at that point solely an expressionless musical
background. It was all a kind of prelude to the actual concert,
whose main piece—at least in my eyes—was supposed to
consist of a permanent and intense screeching from Zorn's
saxophone, which simultaneously being both corrected and
lashed onward (each according to mood) by the other two
instruments, would ultimately end in a classic Zorn inferno
(in an intensive pain of shrilling, embedded in the dignified
background of an insane rhythm of ritual and, with the assistance of the bass, displaced into obliging realms of sound).
All this, however—the crescendo I am speaking about—
never occurred. For some mysterious reason, the concert
was halted after about ten minutes. It was unclear what had
actually happened, in any case it was an abrupt halt. I do
remember that none of the audience protested very much
and they all simply filed out of the hall gradually. My father
and I are still standing there, amazed, lost in thought, as to
what had actually just occurred before our very eyes. From

a room adjacent to the artists dressing room, a long-haired musician emerges (the bass guitarist?) who's slowly 'packing up' individual instruments as if nothing's happened. I felt calmed by the fact that Zorn was alive then and that the collapse that had happened earlier hadn't seriously threatened his health in any way whatsoever. In the very moment that the long-haired fellow went back to the changing area, I caught a glimpse of Zorn, sitting on a wooden chair in guise of a thinker, with a lowered head supported on his hands, visibly recalling the famous Rodin statue. My father was disappointed and said that one just ought not to do such things. Yet suddenly we're also outside, in some desert — no lush vegetation, barely any light — where I patiently explain to my father that nothing's really happened, and above all, that "Zorn surely isn't a junkie", though I'm not as successful in convincing him, nor that he hasn't any sort of alcohol problems like another well known musician we both know well. "He's just a person like any other" I felt the need to point out.

·✢·

But of course, she said, but let's just not turn on this largest one on the ceiling, because it always starts wobbling so much that it looks as if it could fall down right away. Good thing that it's not hanging directly over the bed, I say, and she just laughs. Her two large B's swing above me like bells descending from heaven.

Structuring and blocking.

I remember Martin B., a fellow student from primary school who took the greatest pleasure in observing the bus drivers during the trip from one end station to the other. The investigation of all the particulars and the details that are so indispensable during such a ride. His fascination at the various switches, which the driver would even actually give him sometimes, so many in fact that he already had a complete collection of them at home. Some were black, others white. Like chess figures, like a piano keyboard. A chess figure—a playing object that is capable of engendering calm, a piano keyboard—a playing object that is capable of anything. On and off, yes and no, white and black. The null and the one as principle of a computing device. Computers. What is it we're after during computation? When computing, are we only concerned with the sum? Is the sum the overall number? Of what? What is being calculated here, on an ongoing basis, before our very eyes? Is this a counting off or a counting down?

A Documentary

In a notable documentary film about an aggressive group of football fans in England, filmed by an infiltrator who freely joined this group and whose members he later filmed with a secret camera, we become immediate witnesses to stark, unimaginable scenes which simply shock the viewer in that they depict violence in stark, unposed images, truthfully and without any sort of censorious interference, from the lives of real actors, people whose violence has become an attitude, a pleasure and a form of self expression.

A sad contemplation about a sad topic and all this without anyone bothering to think about it at all. Things happened here.

A certain scene in the film is one I'll never forget. It played out in the emotionally charged surroundings of the local pub where the main character of a senseless—and yet precisely planned—bloodbath directly following a football match of his team somewhere abroad, tells the tale with shining eyes of the sheer delights he experienced when vividly witnessing the cracking of a policeman's breaking spine whom he had beaten with a metal bar, with all his strength, in the presence the policeman's young girlfriend who during the entire 'action' was screaming, terrified . . . While this fellow spoke, he fell into a state of complete ecstacy, one almost had the impression that he had to relive this experience again and again, from the very beginning, this time in the presence of those who understand him, those whom he actually could—and needed to—entrust anything. Entrust? Perhaps even more: Boasting about, proving in the complete steadfastness of his masculine ego that has presented himself, that had satisfied his unquenched longing and until this very moment hadn't been able to get over it. — And yet I could not drive the thought of this bloodthirsty little primate from my memory: "I know that I'm evil, but if I were good, no one would ever remember who I was. *It's because of this* that they'll all remember who I was."

Life's Capability of Bearing Death

The experiences of the dead give us solace whom we, in as much as we acquiesce to them, acquiesce to ourselves, the living. As if it was not true that these dead had once been alive too, as if these dead had never even been alive, or were only alive on account of the same thing whereby they are alive for us today, as the dead. As if the need to bear life, through death, were a generally shared need among the living, to be dead. Equally as it is the *need* of those today, for us living dead, to already be alive for us, while still alive, in reality a need calculated by them in relationship to us — being imaginary for them.

The brief meeting with Pavel and his family — his wife and his three small children — sparked a recollection for me which is indeed quite notoriously known about, which however never ceases to fascinate again and again (and yet at the same time be quite disturbing). This permanent and pitiless need, indeed desire of a child to be noticed accord-

ing to his or her own search for meaningfulness. A child es-
capes no one's notice. A child catches you thinking in every
thought that has nothing to do with him.

Formulating and forming.

·⊹·

It happened during a school trip, how old I was, I can't recall. Sometime during puberty, it seems to me, when I let
this memory to be observed and the point of its appearance
and impact. Let's imagine an instance of ball lightning for
a moment, and along it comes, zipping and clunking, with
no consideration whatsoever for all the heads in front of it.
A kind of socializing that I let myself get talked into playing. Was it badminton? The main thing was that in the
course of playing I really began to sweat and that, much to
my surprise, it went quite well, at least as far as I can remember from the reactions. Actually there were almost ex-
clusively girls playing this game who might have been trying
to drive home some point for me the entire time. Very nice
of them, really nice. That was during the day, in the evening a little TV, and then something forbidden, most likely a little alcohol. I can't remember exactly. I only remember that a fellow student who was always a little bit ahead
of the rest of us came into the TV room just as the film
we'd watched was ending and proceeded to lay out and explain in detail for us what he had just done in one of the
girl's rooms with the class rep. And for us, the inexperienced

ones, there remained no other choice than to listen to the rantings of a more seasoned guy. Quite possible that I had drunk and smoked more than necessary, for by morning I felt so fantastically awful that my whole body began shaking and wouldn't stop. Blood had shot to my hands and finger-tips, was seething and pulsing there, pressing my skin out-wards and forcing my swollen veins toward the surface. The tension in my skin, becoming more & more unbearable by the second, affected a sort of numbness in my hands. I sat down in an armchair, my heart beating frantically, and with the inconspicuous assistance of some fellow students I began conducting small tasks with my hands, such as opening and clenching my fists as fast as possible, for example, which after several patient repetitions showed some effect in that a calm came over me, my blood pressure sinking and the (until that point uninterrupted) tension in my skin subsided. The whole episode, of course, had its little sequel, in the guise of a visit to the local outpatient department in the company of two fellow students who gleefully took advantage of the op-portunity—as my official escorts—to leave and take a seat in one of the local pubs. The doctor, a woman who greet-ed me in between moderate shaking to take my blood pres-sure and run an EKG, was incredibly unsympathetic—but I had no choice in the matter. I think Madame Doctor quite primly enjoyed my fear and I therefore made an even great-er effort to appear 'relaxed'. A few times she tested me with typical school questions (of typical schoolteachers), and then uttered this memorable sentence that will no doubt haunt me for the rest of my life, though it hasn't especially bothered me that I found this line written in black and white in typical schoolbooks for wannabe doctors, which no doctor (even the absolute worst), when preparing to take final exams, with 100 percent certainty (even if he or she wanted to) could dare overlook. That sentence, enunciated in a correspondingly dry manner, was: "If you don't pay closer attention to your blood pressure, you might go blind." Madame Doctor, however, vented this in a pseudo ironic way, "Just be careless, and you shall see!" grinning devilishly.

·╬·

"You will never be able to penetrate Hyde's world," says Hyde to Jekyll. "You'll never be able to penetrate Jekyll's world," says Jekyll to Hyde. And that's exactly what we're talking about here.

·╬·

Another kind of curse that I'll never forget, also from elementary school days, this time directly from the schoolbench (a little scene that played out in the classroom during a break).

I'm not trying to talk myself into thinking that I was any better than any other of the bad kids of my sort, for in truth I really wasn't any better, which I'll admit sometimes made me a little sorry, at least in retrospect, with respect to my parents, whom I really didn't want to cause much sorrow. What was it all about? I don't know anymore what was in my head at the time, I only remember that I set out to hop over the schoolbenches like a frog only to suddenly ambush my chosen 'dearest' and unexpectedly plant a huge kiss on her delicate cheek; obviously as quickly as possible so that she couldn't defend herself. Ha-ha-ha's from the cheap seats, basically from those who considered the observed event as a spectacle. And at that time another one of these lovely young things, with a reproachful glance and the uncompromising presence of a goddess, scathingly stated: "You, YOU'll never find any woman who wants to marry the likes of you!"

⊹

The principle of duplication as opposed to that of singularity. (Singularity fanned out into pluralism, or pluralism united in singularity?)

⊹

The magic of an attic apartment, the magic of loneliness and the need to isolate oneself from the environment which we on the one hand utilize and on the other is fundamentally alien to us. The magic of the possibility of constantly driving necessity way past its outermost fringes, indeed to that point where each step forward invariably represents a boomerang which returns to its starting point, and in so doing properly refers back to it—whether we defend ourselves against it or not.

Every one of us hurtles onward in his or her own way. From a glass encased kitchen balcony of the tiny rooftop apartment on Ben-Yehuda Street directly in the heart of Jerusalem I observe a renter, who, as opposed to me, lives in the lowest ground floor apartment, from which window he — this lively, bald-headed renter — hangs his colorful washing on secured drying stands, which seems to me as if he were simultaneously playing the maidservant, the housekeeper and the housewife. Could it be that this sort of apartment (actually calling it a single family home might be more fitting, kind of a little snail's house, even with a little flight of stairs at the entryway located on the inner courtyard side) was actually automatically connected (in my perception) with a larger family, indeed with an environment where naturally an actual female housekeeper would also be present?

I had moved into my miniature apartment after my harsh split with N., which didn't prevent me from staying in this (now as before) foreign land. And so I wondered what could have moved my clearly much senior neighbor to move to such a bizarre location on one of the main streets in the city. Actually I often asked myself the question whether or not there were brothels here, in the Holy City, for if not, it certainly would have been very unusual. One afternoon, on a holiday, or shortly before one, for a deathly silence pervaded the place everywhere, a singular sight played out beneath my kitchen window. It may be possible that this particular lady remained ensnared in my memory because of how she just happened to straighten herself up right before the entryway, and then perhaps also because of the whole elegance of her bodily tenseness, when she, in a black, skintight slip, in the air that was becoming stickier by the second, no soul in sight left or right, slowly but surely tapped out her secret code with her heel on the pavement that had been devised for this moment alone.

·✠·

Irreproachable tenderness.

Analyzing and catalyzing.

Unbleeding.

Connecting into the never before interconnected?

And throughout the expulsion process, arriving quite obviously at exclusivity.

·✠·

Martin P., who was in the habit of using the nickname of Kato, had always fascinated me thanks to the considered distance he kept from others as well as his ability to keep things blithely at bay, which, especially during communist times, was of undeniable advantage. The amazing diversity of his collection of dried marihuana fascinated me, of which he (according to his own reports) stored thirty or so types—

"the right one for every mood." This seemed remarkable to me. Later I myself accumulated quite a collection of albums, CDs and books so that, God willing, none of my moods could take me by surprise. But from this situation arose another problem that consisted of a certain obtuseness and the incapability of sensing something like a mood at all, without knowing exactly which compartment to sort that mood into. And this compelled me to expand the number of boxes—and with it the entire collection—proportionally to the increase of perceptions of the dispersion of the possibilities to fathom that which, of all that I thought I was perceiving, perceived as . . . worth acknowledging. For anything else beyond this was simply drowned in an alcoholic stupor back then.

⁘

It is much more necessary to comprehend the procedural character of my thinking than its immovability. Traveling through a dark tunnel without imagining a light at its end is both absurd and idiotic.

It is necessary . . .

Ridding oneself of the necessity for objectivity is therefore quite necessary because objectivity is never the object of a necessity.

⁘

Individuals write in order not to forget, and through writing they summon the memory. The question is, in so doing, what is summoned, the question is whether or not memory is ever truly complete. In summoning from the memory, do we not always call forth from memory that which is absent in it? Is not the summoning from the memory of that which has been summoned the reverse reconstruction of the memory—and thus, in fact, its construction? And what of that which we've summoned forth from our memory, what belongs to memory and what belongs to the summoning? Does memory have a spirit? If so, is this spirit then directly connected to memory or is it subsequently implanted through the spirit of that individual who has called for this spirit? Are we not in fact talking about a kind of spiritual incantation?

June 10, 2005

In the evening the day before yesterday, I had a meeting with Viktor K. who had promised to make me a perfect digital portrait. Through the entire sitting, which for me was really quite pleasant, I suspected (and saw it later in the camera's viewfinder quite clearly) that Viktor K., a photographer, both in my absence in his eye—yet, in reality, in my presence—had manipulated my picture, was trying to force me into a certain kind of presentation, and in so doing had basically taken me prisoner. The generally decadent atmosphere of the pictures only sparsely affected the visually pronounced movements of overdone gestures, all in the middle of a hallway filled with artificial fog and well-placed little tables that were illuminated by means of subtle lighting shining down from the ceiling in red columns. Later we both dubbed this 'a demonic game' and mutually reassured each other that this hadn't been the right way to go about it. Finally, however, after about fifty clicks and a liter of wine, we managed to get a good take. Yesterday I mailed this on to J., curious as to his opinion. J. answered that he liked the picture and I (aside from the new, slight double chin) looked just like a child. Since this time the question has plagued me whether or not that demon within me doesn't have something deep and significant in common with this child…

⯎

A child cannot love, for it doesn't know what it means not being able to.

To be like a child, at least for a moment. To *be able* to be a child . . .

Vitalization, or cauterization?

The bottom as an inversion of a summit—a summit, too.

Heavens induced anxiety, screaming into the heavens.

⯎

Through the view of light, through the view of darkness.

The weight of 'years' casts its weight onto the scale, in case the reason for getting old were this one alone. The weight answering a question regarding weightiness, poses the question as to the weightiness of the scale. Time, internalized by experiences, passes flowingly, painlessly, into eternity.

My favorite park in Jerusalem; benches secured to the ground, women with children and me with Nietzsche.

Prayers and incantations.

Overreduction.

⁜

What is exactly being tested with litmus? The equivalent characteristics of that which is tested, sorted to this or that color of the testing paper, or the characteristics of the litmus itself, whose characteristic it is, in this way or that (depending on the appearance of that which is being tested), to color the little paper that is testing the said characteristics?

And he who is seeking identity seeks the identity of that which he is seeking.

Through burial rights.

Supposedly, Streicher would sit, while composing his anti-Jewish pamphlets, naked at his desk, and apparently it aroused him a good deal . . .

Unimaginable. Unfeelable. Not to drive a thought home. Not to feel through to the end.

And then there's this deceptive word 'self-realization', for who can self-realize?

·╬·

Image No. 1

A glass windowed cafe at Astor Place in New York. A long-haired fellow who, day after day, sat for hours on end with a cardboard cupped *tall coffee* at the little table next to the outlet in front of a laptop and a high stack of blank CDs, slumped forward, systematically burning one after the other with music from his youth.

Image No. 2

The singer from Pink Floyd, taking a walk across the Charles Bridge in Prague with his beautiful, dreamy girlfriend.

He only observes that which he sees and only sees that which he observes:

Clenched-teeth thoughts, formulated with clenched teeth.

A legitimate crime of a legitimate punishment.

Looking, consistently chiseled in the form of that which is seen.

·✦·

The Story of N.

1

The worst thing is that N. is constantly trying to play the demagogue, which in a bigger crowd tends to make big impressions. In especially charged situations there's simply no other way, especially when other people who are clearly partial to N. are gathered about, listening. It bothers me to be a societal lines-cracking machine which they, P. and others would like to have in me — so that they might confirm their ideas about how I'm supposed to appear in their presence. They turn me into a circus monkey, which is at a minimum a kind of manipulation, pampering laboriously an occasion here and there wherein I'm supposed to play the actor at their little cues. And sometimes they manage to stumble in (not them, just N., with her cheap, overdone laugh) during necessary pauses in the discussion which unmistakenly arise because of that aforementioned demagoguery. In short: It's a vicious circle of a psychotic game that becomes more and more aggressive and leads to an utter split-up of the group.

2

That she irritates me is actually quite inspiring . . .

3

She fully ensnared P., and he sucks her like a piece of candy. Once he commented about her: "I feel like I've been hatched from you."

4

I'm considering on what basis I could actually speak in this way about her. She says: I'm a mirror. But what isn't she, actually? Does this sentence not include the prerequisite condition of a one-sided, permeable mirror, behind which SHE is standing?

5

"These little fingers of yours," she says, allowing them to glide across her delicate, extended throat.

6

A typical misunderstanding: I stick my tongue out, she tickles with her tongue.

7

I allow myself to be enraptured, and to enrapture, too. Nothing inbetween . . .

8

A dead evening at the cafe. Silent tension between M. and me, lasting something like an hour. Then M. gets up and disappears, proudly, without even saying good-bye. I amble through the streets. I call P. A whisper responds: "I'm already asleep . . ." "Sorry," I answer, "maybe some other time."— "Robert!" someone shouts from behind, a familiar female voice and interrupts my thoughts, already in motion with respect to the lack of lettuce in my two hamburgers, from neither of which I've yet been able to take a bite. Of course it's N., "Sorceress, look at you! You're all dressed up . . . in black, today" I say, accompanied by a gesture something similar to waving a wand (or a whip). "Me, and a sorceress?" "No, it's YOU that's the sorcerer . . ." she replies and disappears into the depths of the night. I just barely manage to stroke her right cheek in the process. I don't look at her and yet feel, quite subtly, the extending of my member to an erection.

So frail that every internal cause (shove?) becomes an instigation to a 'new beginning' for him.

Two Images

1. The image of a young gypsy on the bus (how old was I? thirteen?) who displays the undersides of his eyeballs, their whiteness streaked with the slightly protruding veins, "which are blind," pressing two of his fingers under the eye sockets.

2. The long-lasting, horrid scene of a murder from Kieślowski's *Short Film about Killing* which caused me such a feeling of disgust that I was forced to leave the cinema (when was that? thirteen years ago?).

Something which couldn't be seen in the recollection of looking beyond inward (image 1), got connected in my head with the idea of unimagineable pain and blood—of its essence—that is linked to the former and bubbles somewhere within it (image 2).

"Papa, you're a scientist, right?" I shouted up to the seventh floor window from below. As if the kids didn't believe me? Why shouldn't they have? Did this reality seem relevant to them in any way at all? What would have happened if father had denied this at that very moment—what would have happened in my mind, or his?

And then there are the two stories about pissing. The one, it's already been ages since that happened, sometime during the last days of elementary school. There was a celebration and everyone was drinking something or other. Then I went home with one of our schoolmates and along the way I had the urge to go. I held it almost to the front door, but then, for some reason quite unknown to me, I sprang into the basement where I relieved myself unceremoniously next to a hydrant. Nothing would have happened if not for one of the neighbors who, thanks to the sound of liquid trickling from an unknown source, stepped out to the landing and turned on the light. What happened then I can only recall vaguely. I know for sure that I had gravely insulted this gentleman in that I, having finished peeing next to his apartment door, clumsily bleated in a state of drunkenness that he, my friend's neighbor, who dared in his very house to burden me with reference to my impudence "must not know who my father is". (I have no idea whether or not he grabbed me by the ear, in any case this sort of boxing of the ears didn't seem likely, as I recalled it. Or the observation that I spat at him.)

And then we have the infamous Brooklyn story, where I landed in a holding cell in handcuffs, the first—and luckily only—real criminal incident in my life. It had to do with this feeling of independence (freedom), to do with the feeling of being in New York, just as I was returning home at about 2 a.m. after a fine evening. Naturally I thought I could gleefully pee wherever I wanted to, especially after all the restaurants where I might have chosen to go to the bathroom had long since closed. So there I am, standing at the corner of a building when suddenly, out of nowhere, the bright light of a flashlight hits me in the face—sneaky, since coming from behind, it can't be detected and there's no one stopping it. And it was a beat cop's flashlight that had caught me in the act, or at least engaging in an activity that seemed like an 'incident' for the bored Brooklyn cops. They asked me to get in the car and after I had sputtered in my broken English that any dog would be allowed to do the thing they wanted to hold me for, and when I gestured a bit too excitedly while explaining this fact, they put the cuffs on me, just in case. Contributing to the tragicomic moment was the presence of a stuttering intellectual from the Polish movement, who was in a state of complete despair and had no idea what to say or how to react to all of this. Ultimately it was a good thing he was present, since he could at least be my witness (for otherwise I might well have been lynched for this kind of behavior). I saw him, still in a state of disbelief, moving off somewhere from where the police car later brought me, only from the other side, the whole thing playing out in an area something like 50 to 100 square meters— proof positive that my hypothesis about the police being bored was a correct one after all.

Wait, where did all this begin? "Don't you know who my father is?" Shut up already, what's that got to do with the here and now, in Brooklyn . . .

⊹

The brief meeting with Pavel and his family—the wife and the three small children—reminded me of the following, also. Everyone was hurrying (and especially the oldest of the sons, who was truly excited and honestly fascinated), they all ran home just so they wouldn't miss Papa, who was going to be on television.

A thermometer doesn't feel warmth (or coldness), just as a musical instrument doesn't feel music.

And then the nights of those who so mask their sadness that they no longer even recognize it. "Are you happy? Are you truly happy now?" the victim of his brief inquiry asks in badly phrased English, drunk, sitting on his knees in the tram, questioning in badly phrased English, questioning who really can turn into anything other than this. So, indeed, he gets dressed, so nothing old will be sticking out, puts on an act for some girl, who's desperately trying to forget something, in vain. She's at his disposal today. She allows herself to be carried to his lair, and he may do as he wishes. What twists or turns could possibly be in store now? Love? These two don't even speak to each other anymore, just listening to the muffled screams from someplace, from where is always better for one to escape, even though (and that's exactly what we're concerned with here) there is nowhere to go. He might play the 'nice uncle' or 'turn her over' with the girl, who is just happy to be of some sort of service to someone for a little while, so that she can say afterwards, yes, I'm good, I've done what I can in order to know what it means to love, to forgive, to be benevolent and helpful to forget. Helping and forgetting.

⁘

And yet again several disparate things came together to form an image. I was permitted to prepare more properly than any other of these sorts of ceremonies, for in this case, we can also consider a typical evening meal as a kind of ceremony—even the invitation to dinner as such. Aside from this we also received the special note that one should prepare properly for this event, both in terms of personal gear as well as the munitions for the evening. Naturally in so saying I am referring to the suits, capes and the like, referred to generally as clothes. Actually, this was all quite convenient for me, for at least now I would have a reason to propose that my old friend Lenka K. take a little time to go with me to the Barrandov Film Studio, for one of the directives of that 'special request' was that only clothes from the 1920s were permitted, which one can only usually scare up from film or theatre shops. And this seemed an especially ideal circumstance to experience something interesting, and accompanied by a person whose presence always seemed to induce a certain state of intoxication in me, indeed, in a certain way, similar to a kind of drug high, even if I really didn't personally know all that much about what these states actually feel like. Luckily.

I first met Lenka K. in the local film club, wait, no, actually we never would have met there. I don't count myself among the ranks of those who end up approaching the one they've been eyeing, say "A . . ." and then have her. No, I can go on ardently observing the object of my desire for years without even saying "B . . ." But what does it matter. Basically this city is the asshole of the world as we all know too well, so that ultimately everyone meets everyone else and we can quietly play out our little games in any direction we choose, knowing well that everyone foresees the end of their paths somewhere else anyway, so that where one path is beginning, the other ends, or something like to that effect. It's a kind of group sex of intentions, of which some constantly inter-sect—those are the parallels—and some, now and again, bump into each other and then quickly part ways. And then there are those that quite intentionally smash into each other, and from these spring forth great loves, and great hatreds. And quite possibly even great indifferences, only much later. But let's return to Lenka K.

So, the first thing that attracted me was certainly the most visible, that which unacknowledged could not be perceived in any other way, than a blatant ignorance to the visible, for how could one encounter the unseen if one doesn't see any of it. It is good to see something, to lean on it, to base one's impression upon it and move forward in a measured way, step-by-step, focusing in upon it all the more precisely— and either to confirm it, step-by-step (which may also take some years), or ultimately rebuke it. The greater the effect of the first impression, all the stronger are the observer's mental ties to that which is observed, whatever the former and the latter might stand for. This is a truth that every impression-maker knows full well, which everyone who creates an impression knows full well about. Every impression-maker is unconsciously aware of the fact that he or she generates a conscious impression with it — an impression through which the impression-maker enters into the consciousness of conscious individuals, who in turn succumb to an impression. What we're talking about here is this: One is the maker, and one is the consumer; one has the obligation to the other to dish up something or other and the other is then obligated to gobble it up. In that moment when it comes to the 'gobbling' we may well say: The game is afoot! For the first thing we're always considering here is the latent, present moment of the game which, however, in order to be made manifest, must be initiated in some way.

We all ran into each other — quite by chance — in the dressing room of the costume shop. What had suddenly become of us all? Who among us back then was there as themselves, and who on the basis of an ideal image of themselves that they desperately wanted to project? Lenka K., who, in the years that I had known her had only ever appeared in black, suddenly shone in a bright orange like a shining corona. She looked at me: "So, what do you think, does it look good on me?" The fatality that accompanied her words was so compelling, so conquering that I really had to make a double effort not to betray my emotional sensitivity and to note in passing: "Yes, you look fabulous in that," and while saying it, put on a deadpanned face, much as if it was part of my daily routine to evaluate the charm of the most seductive of women.

Ultimately the others also seeking outfits also praised her loveliness, those characters I knew well from the late night bars and cafes, who at this midday hour appeared much as metamorphized, groping figures who at the same time were trying their best not to betray their frailties which during *their* hours would effortlessly disappear, transforming to those good old spirits, those good old werewolves that I knew so well.

Ben N., the future husband-to-be, constantly babied by his future better half, tried on one suit after the other, only to ultimately decide on something quite unconventional; it was a gold edged samurai kimono, which he topped off with a musketeer hat, giving me the decided impression that he had a sword in his hand—just in case it might be necessary to actually *strike off* something to someone.

The demonic character of his enthusiasm and how he stood before the mirror in this costume (which this first mirror as in the transmitted sense his future wife and his band of friends comprised) struck me visually to an even greater extent than the withdrawn attitude of his future female half at this very moment, who of the two, perhaps saw herself the more masculine of the two halves.

In the end, we didn't even get a chance to experience the wedding ceremony, for the whole masquerade was only an evening invitation to the wedding reception — or at least we perceived it to be so. I was freaked out the whole day through, didn't eat at all, even forgetting the wedding gift at home. It was a picture that had hung on my wall at home for years and to which I had developed something of an emotional connection, regardless the fact that the painter was well known as a pedophile in artists' circles (which doesn't mean all that much) throughout Bratislava.

I had to return for the picture while she waited for me in a tasteless (yet in its own way quite charming) cafe. I can well imagine how she sat there at the time, drinking something, her raven black hair dropping to table's edge. I returned in about half an hour and then we downed a few shots of whiskey — partly out of the shared excitement about each other, about the wedding and even about the picture — to kill off the stage fright, as it were.

At the reception, where we had arrived after a while, canopies throned the festive little trays, and since it was somewhat embarassing to clear them aside into piles, ultimately both of us — especially *me* — failed to eat a thing. The happy couple barely took notice of us and didn't even cast a single glance at the picture. On one occasion, when I accidentally distanced myself from Lenka, a local lunatic we all knew very well immediately graced her with his attentions, explaining to her hurriedly how truly successful he *re-*

ally was in life. Once again the demonic personage of the
now young husband struck me then and I took the liberty to
share this impression with Lenka, who related, however, that
she found nothing demonic whatsoever about him. After
standing around for about one or two hours hopeless hours
on a spot where time stood still, we all took refuge in a pub
in which we could finally fill our stomachs—or at least *I*
certainly did. Suddenly I stood up and left my beauty behind that day, exceptionally outfitted in orange (but today,
today she's wearing black again!), sitting at one of the elevat-
ed tables—just where I'd once been in the habit of sitting
with an ex girlfriend—in the company of some unknown
surrealists, who didn't interest me in the least at that moment. I quickly left the place without saying good-bye and
she, Lenka, believe it or not, ran after me in the end: And
we embraced. It was an unusual embrace, during which I
sensed her immense tenderness and at the same time, equally, the great need to be the one who's protected. And this
just simply clobbered me. Walking on a few meters—luckily she saw nothing—I had to puke my guts out.

My life: A lecture, to be continued . . .

Not to declame, but to convey.

Self—a Demiurge, or a Demiurge—Nature?

Contexts of closure.

·✢·

Lenka K. and myself. She always sits in the farthest corner
of the movie theatre, in the outcrop directly behind the door
(so she can come late and leave early if need be), and I'm always the last one to leave the bar or an evening get together
with friends (at a minimum to be sure that while present no-
body's talking about me behind my back).

·✢·

"The movement of sculpture" as a permanent attempt to ex-
ecute a dance step.

Weakness, that fascinates.

The spiritual element of emotional imbalance.

From eternity into eternity.

Not being able to desire, or not having to have to?

(I employ) another design for living.

Taboo and not taboo.

The fricative surfaces of delight.

Gas-mascots.

To be inclined to the truth and to be inclined to the lie. Check to what extent the lie lies — from the viewpoint of the truth? I don't believe that. The lie, consistently and inevitably masked (in order to remain inscrutable), which surfaces "at the first glance" in some unexpected moment. Hence, momentarily, a snapshot in time: Click! And that's it.

The word — a spot on the paper. Is note-taking anything other than blemishing?

In the park today, two women screamed to each other: *Alice! Peter!* and in so doing, meant their children.

Tragicoma.

For whom the necessity of the podium represents the necessity of a performance. For what might it mean for those we're speaking about here *not* to step out from within? And this is where the very difference between a performance and a position exists. For an actor can never stand behind that which he is presenting. Though a politician, a public representative, etc.

Sacrificing life unto the sacrifice of life?

Self-assaulting mind.

Monotypes I

Immortally young, immortally old. Immortally . . .

This fine, bronze hair, as long as waiting for *the* moment which they would fit into, permeated by a glowing bundle of light, shining through the flamethrower of the setting sun over a bridge across the Moldau. This hair, at the same time meaning that beauty is a creation of the moment which every second is just so complete and full, in order to be full, at every moment in time, *always* and *just* and in such a fashion that it should never get to its extreme edge — for reaching the extreme means being repelled from that — which to think it already means bordering on it, yet it has no border at all, it is always located, from the very first moment, just behind this border which it neither has within nor outside of itself.

Developing and escaping.

"One sees" is simply invisible.

Life incompetence.

Monotypes II

The human element that is constantly shunted to the edge in order not to hinder flights of fancy. In so doing, woman is always the most human. Woman, that with age becomes all the more so . . .

The instrumentalization in the execution of the punishment with respect to its opposite, to enthusiasm.

For acts and activities.

Children's crying which becomes all the more pronounced, and the more pronounced it becomes, only to ultimately discharge into a sudden game of love between archetypal cats.

Beneath the burden of wings.

Monotypes III

My life's experience is so unique that it's almost impossible to find someone with one that's comparable. The question is, where is it written that somebody has to look for someone like this? Not to mention the fact that seeking *the one* could simply mean finding *the other* . . . If, however, to find oneness in oneself means to find a self in one—does this not simultaneously mean that there's no room for the other?

The less filth there is, the easier it is to see.

Silence, remaining silent.

Ladislav K., a well known philosopher in the post-Nietzs-
chean tradition who, following intensive study of the so-
called divine essence ultimately arrived at the ingenious con-
clusion: "I am not God, no!" was not influenced as much
by the thoroughness of his studies as so much more by the
intensity and persistence of his toothaches . . .

The aura that summons the spirit from the fog.

Monotypes IV

One stalked during a walk through the park, the other
chased by the pursuer right up to her front door. The third
hadn't come yet, though she's already waiting for the moment (even if she herself isn't aware of it) when everyone
would change roles.

Every denomination is renaming.

The temptation of the game is—like every temptation—
a gift whose acceptance means succumbing to it, and what
(scandalous thing or other) we can expect to find in it. Only
the motivation that actually summoned it forth can multi-
ply its effect. Blood flows back to the source.

That which I live, and that which I die.

Enticement, unto the earth.

Monotypes V

That need "to solve a problem," summoned forth through the consistent generation of a structure that by necessity joins the form of the problem itself. In case one doesn't see a problem, this means that the structure was not properly formed. (In the case that there's no structure whatsoever possessing the ability to generate itself, in which that which is able to be generated from it simply remains unrecognizable.)

Observers and observed and observers that, in an uncontrolled moment, *happen to be observed* . . .

Condensation of contemplation.

The farther, the less . . . up to a point . . . and even that is first a thought.

Antiretouching.

⊹

July 3, 2005

Today, after getting up, I found a dead young dove on the balcony. His innards, blood-red and turned inside-out, along with his feathers, strewn about, indicated that this animal's departure from this world very probably unfolded in a very dramatic manner. I immediately connected this event to the death of a poet, the facts of which I had learned about just a few days prior, more than ten years after his demise. On the window ledge from which the talented fellow had jumped, visible scratch marks were discovered which his fingers had left behind as he had with all probability attempted to raise his body up again and prevent his drop from the ninth floor, for most likely the poet had reconsidered his choice at the final moment.

⁜

Pressing Onwards, unto the Substance of Requiring

Riding the bike down the hill, and the facilitated incision through the air. Initially somewhat painful, recognition of body (pressing down on the pedals), and then (coasting) in a pure ecstasy of relinquishment, of allowing one to drop into unknown depths to the point where the hill naturally leads, on its own, since it is downhill. Meanwhile, all the fluids (sweated out) get absorbed, with the pleasant coolness enveloping his upper body, back into the skin. The descent and all the released tensions that in the constrained climb of the hill had been mounting.

The biology teachers' assignments: the plant herbarium, colorful butterfly wings that lose nothing in being pressed, much the opposite … The teacher knew how to enjoy the systematic nature of it all, no doubt about it. Her attentive glance: observant. The glance of her eyes behind gold-framed glasses, the glance behind her eyes … Her attentive glance and strict cadence of her voice in the class when we dissected the frog …

Each of us cut from our mother twin at the umbilical cord. From the twin of the mother and the father, from the twin of the mother and the father and the holy spirit. Amen.

And then there are these extravagant colors, as if she wanted to say "now here I come, the red" … She screamed something at me, actually we cancelled each other out screaming over the top of each other … Until a howling police van interceded, from which I was forced to run, *as if it were before her* … She, the extractor of private information, according to which the end of the world (which is ultimately the subject here) depends on a specific sum of specific sorrows that she alone is able to accumulate.

Still, crying about the closeness of suffering, not for he who *suffers*, but for *he* who suffers . . .

Holocasts.

Searching for a Place

The one or the other side, for there's only one. Briefly, it's not possible to be unsided, we're talking about the attraction of one of the two sides, we're talking about the repelling of the other that we know. For the unknown cannot be repelling . . . The impossibility of the one, and therefore the necessity of the other. *And therefore*, and thereby the other . . .

He put her to my ear, the receiver, emanating with her breath, and in so doing breathed life in. . . Was there really any further amount of imagination required of me with respect to this . . . ? A year later she would perform a little good-night dance for me, the good fairy. A year later . . .

But all that had already begun much, much earlier. On the wooden pier, by the lake, at sundown. A kind of sorrow, both petition and prayer that were reflected so purely and sincerely in her twelve-year-old eyes that it almost made me sorry to be aware of it all, and to caution myself constantly: Just don't surrender to sentimentality!

Transfigured night, in the face, or perhaps solely a spark of it. Un-figured-out.

Experiencing this once again from the beginning, undisturbed by its own distracting lines, that in turn disturb it.

That bit from childhood — what. The revitalized.

When loosening up, one means removing the loosening from the other.

Interactive screaming.

Looking for the place within, towards the other. Looking for the place within, the other *towards oneself in them*.

Interactive Silence

A stillness that is initially a stillness ready to be, once it ceases to be still ... An end, recurring so many times that in the moment that it ends ... An ignited fire of the end to an extent of necessary measure ... A braided braid ... Getting to know one another and being known ... In the trap of mental unification ... Nonbreak-down ... Silence, sounded over, blaspheming about silence and about not being silent ... The inability to locate the word, and yet the necessity to seek it, as if the word could save one from that which is unsaid.

Personalities

The entirety of the face, *all for one* ... Whatever happens, happens ... The catastrophic scenario of an acknowledged catastrophe ... At first glance we can always see the following ... We consider the unthinkable. In blurring out associations we create associations ... For none of us is so isolated from others, we all run into one another, even if we never do.

That which I feel and that which I turn feelingless ... A strike to the innermost ... Entering the stage from the still open ground, for a defense.

Stepping in action on the basis of an opportunity?

⸭

The naturally despairing need to grasp before we lose it ... It almost looks as if we are taking each other over, in turns ... And during all this, we hear the bursting din of the waves: a sound deadening attentiveness ... And yet we're concerned here with a certain kind of coordination, with a commitment, a trip, and even a breaking out from a productive medley of interactive energies, whereever its core may be.

All together, with chess board and figures.

Outer displays of the internal.

Retrospectrum.

⊹

Polite words that don't even pretend to mask their disinterestedness, that yield to the free flow of words, no longer a story because this story is no longer necessary. They have long since absolved themselves of their story for us. They no longer find it necessary to pretend to have an impression of communicability, which in this case couldn't be communicated in any other than a one-sided manner, indeed, not at all. Yet even we begin to slowly comprehend it all. Even we demand from the others not that which means doubting the right, but having the right to do so. And so on. So everything is quite in order here. There's no reason to push back from this side or the other. Complete understanding.

⊹

And then the mechanism of expression of a need that "is being executed."

Words concealing meaning which conceals words that conceal meaning . . .

The internalization of the internal.

Undifferentiality of one from the other, where the one is inserted in the other.

An eye's split with an eye.

Impotential

That which we let come in and that which we never allow to enter. The flood of words. The word, like smoke. Always too late. Always already different. The word as a question, not to be posed, the word as an answer, not even given. The word as the only possible testimony, always unquestioned. The fracture, unable to be prepared, always ready to speak out. The fracture of the heart that, cut out of itself, still feels.

Uninfinity.

Unto the magnitude of the possibility of salvation of salvation.

The penetration of sorrow ... A heart, cut in half ... A massacre of causal connections ... Contamination of feelings ... The contracted easing in relief at eternity, to be continued.

... but eternity knows no continuation.

The Construction of Memory

Ben N.: "When in Japan, we do this ... but when I'm in Prague ..." He comes here for a few days, on a jaunt from Tokyo, to visit friends and his wife (who's still finishing university), here without work and there living with mother but at least with a roof over his head. "When my mother wakes me in the morning she raises the curtains and talks to me, always forgetting (Mami, please!) that I don't go to bed until near sunrise anyhow ... and I put the pillow over my head and press it down tightly on all sides ..." And how's the Tokyo club scene, the girls, I ask. "There are pretty musicians that you can have a drink with after the concerts and talk a bit ..." He says: "This bar hasn't changed much ..." We drink a dark beer together and observe a comely dark sorceress behind the bar. "Your wife's still fast asleep, right?" I can't resist asking.

The recallibration of perceptions, a constant supercollision ... A coincident ... Phantomization, a formaldehyde of structure ... Neology.

"The hell in your eyes," but every person seeking that which *he* seeks.

You are saying something. I watch the rhythmic parting and closing of your better lip half, the rhythmic pulse of the machinery of your body, whose hidden parts can be recognized, even beneath the layers that conceal its bareness. Lips that belong to a body and at the same time (in what they say) transcend it. Lips that alone, in saying what they are saying . . .

The hostility of the unusual.

Pleonazism.

⊹

Memory is always complete up to that point in time in which something is retrieved from it. Then, all words are in queue, shrewdly connected, in a chain of associations that we summarily designate as reality. A reality that yields a summarizing image of wholeness, which solely exists as such, however, in the memory, for without it, its only justification for existing would be in its own fleetingness, which is intangible.

Necrology

The urgent eyes of a glance that inevitably is one-directional, since it isn't prepared to receive anything more than a confirmation. A glance, that is only sent when it has received another glance beforehand, a glance which transmits through an act of draining. A glance that already knows, because it no longer seeks. An ignited glance, of withered eyes.

An act, seeking its essence.

Language as a means of speaking, and language as a means of the speaking of language.

Fate-formation . . . Surfaces leveling . . . Wing mounting . . .

Unto the immortality of one's part.

Depardoning

The urgent need to speak out, solely concealing the even greater need to be silent . . . Yet how can anyone be silent when there are so many understanding eyes surrounding us everywhere, so many tiny lakes into which one could jump . . . Whatever the sense of this game may be, the means that it sanctifies cannot but stand in opposition to it.

Deep into the night and right up to the break of day, the direction of the finite. On knees . . .

Condensed coma of clarification . . . Co-memoria . . . Casuistry of a cavity.

The era of eternity.

Factologic.

Encryption

"From an inner drive ..." Yet what is it that drives from within? To what extent is that which drives from within, the constant of the drive, that's located within? Is that which is within *driven* from within? If so, from which within? Is there something like an internal disposition to the internal drive?

Eruptionality.

Every step on earth leads to the ground.

A falling as a result of depth, or a depth as a result of a falling?

Life—everything that was not caused.

Living Immediacy

With an entreaty in the eyes—what with all the exuberance—since hung by the wings off the rod of curiosity. The wings constrained by flight (in turn, supporting them).

The focusing of the eyes. One look falls to the others. Hopeless.

Another girl whose mother (mother?) relentlessly repeats: "She's respectable!"

A sideways glance and a glance which screws one's ways.

Corkscrews. Wine, open. The same wine, all over again.

A Cabbalist who has no idea about Cabbala.

Through one's own agency, but without effect.

Spiritworks

Spiritual purification and a concern for the soul, that it remains pure.

And pain as *the* concern of a generation?

She expressed her gratitude for the things she had not experienced with me.

Every truth is an experiment.

The mapping of the world which divided the world into a mapped out world, and a world map.

Approximation of aggression.

Root-uprooters.

PART TWO

Encoding

Nietzsche divides artists into two groups, one that creates from surplus and the other that creates out of privation. It does occur now and again, however, that surplus can represent a form of privation—and this is definitely the case when it comes to obsession.

The Devil's creative power, or the loyalty of God to the created?

Immobilizing.

·✦·

And that 'normal, all too normal' which taxes the normality of absent excessiveness. (Yet when is the measure of excess enough, and what does it suffice for then? Doesn't our problem rather lie in the fact that we unconsciously confuse normality with *normativity*)?

The formalization of the informal by stating: "this is going to be informal."

Decommunication.

Physical pain is more defined, emotional pain the more abstract. In order to sense it, one needs powers of imagination, indeed, in a direct correlation of one to the other. This leads to the question of the functionality of this relationship to an experiencing as such . . .

Openness, bordering on deflation.

Ethics as an aesthetic category (this or that "would be nice" to do).

Hatching life like an egg.

She thanked me for what she had witnessed in my presence. Whatever this "in my presence" might mean. In a way, she didn't know what she was saying, but then again, maybe she did. For the thought that someone might have expected even something else from her didn't really occur to her. For she was driven by her greed to continually interpret the world as though the latter couldn't have been permitted to remain uninterpreted. Every step, in whatever direction, in this case amounted to an act of unlocking, a key to a door that her powers of imagination had to see behind each and every one of these types of steps. For how else could one unlock ideas, if not precisely through the agency of imagination?

Students, fascinated by female teachers.

It's quite easy to recognize the fact that, in the metaphor of the broken heart, the parallels drawn between man and machine are in no way unfounded.

A spiritualized body, and a body enamoured within a soul.

Protologically.

"We loved each other, but didn't like each other."

⊹

September 17, 2005

I went past that cherished bench in Jerusalem where many years before I had churned through Nietzsche and Cioran and wrote later — in the course of a few days — the first part of my *Signs and Symptoms*. I wanted to sit down for a bit and recall that time when I suddenly noticed, on the same bench, a young intellectual of about my age at that time, sitting and delving through the pages of a book by some philosopher or other. In passing, I noticed how he had marked out a few lines with a highlighter. It perhaps surprised the young fellow that I walked past and then, shortly thereafter, turned and came back. We quickly noticed each other. This exchange of glances seemed meaningful to me . . .

The life-long battle with one's whole life.

Unachievements.

The shining eyes of seemingly unapparent protectors of order, duly donning their masks of servility.

The real can solely interest us humans as a curiosity, never as something that anyone can seriously rely on. Thus the efforts on the part of intelligent heads to determine such a concept of reality . . .

Enough of tenderness! her eyes seem to say preventively.

Centerpointing.

⁘

A classic image: She kisses him and he looks to see how people are looking at them.

    A
Nirvanization.
Sorting out the sporadic.
Undeception.
The transparency of sorrow.
Unexbirthed.

B
Deshadowing.
The cult of culture and cultivation.
Intemporation.
Laughing as a resonance of the fall.
Antigony.

C
What's a toxic time.
The presumption of innocence.
Teasing limits simply because limits tease us?
Exterritories, a potential for the past.
Preproduction.

It concerns a certain kind of walk, in our case a form of fix-ation. If possible, one must choose as least subordinated as possible that which fixes—whether dealing with shoes or another, more or less functional component of a fashion outfit.

A fixation on what was, naturally growing into a fixation on what could be.

⊹

They wouldn't let him in, but only not there, where he's just entered. Did he have to enter someplace so THEY wouldn't let him in? They dissected him, in fact, into the past, into the components of a non-existent machine that most likely had never existed before. He was there as a counter-point to them, though; to what other ends would it otherwise have been necessary to enter into them. To enter into them for the purpose of entering into himself, with the act being repeated again and again. If he, in those moments of permanent severances—which occurred permanently—had delved into contemplation rather than acting, he would have long since been somewhere else. Yet he was a man of action: the obstructions to that, which he was not, he squelched by being the way he was. Without any sort of interspacing that arises through a distance of the actor to the act, without any sort of overhyped belief in the possibility of this act. In actuality he was behaving—from the standpoint of Reason—completely irrationally. Yet Reason could have no complaints as far as his behavior was concerned, for in reasonable moments, it was preoccupied with itself and enjoyed it all the while. Reason became the father of all his creations so that the awareness of its absence could become the mother of all his antics. He only chided them always with that which he would never deny within himself. He didn't bother at all to try to discover through what he theoretically was, but he also didn't relinquish his theoretical efforts to those so that theory would keep him down. He strove to be a sovereign bearer of a sovereign feeling in himself. Ultimately he managed to get stuck—relatively luckily—in a comparatively happy marriage. Since then he is invisible. Only here and there he gets a book published, documenting the next stage of his journey, not of much interest to me and my kind of people.

⁘

The need to enlighten, from which stems the need for light, and the need of light from which stems the need to enlighten.

Private idioms combating reality.

Argumentality.

Severance with every break, with every break the functional, that's coming.

Cadaster of catastrophies.

A stronghead.

Time's overcontraction, which loses the need to draw together, one time contaminating the other. Not even eternity is solace anymore and even that must be well timed nowadays. Which is the time that ceases to be eternal, continuing through rupture.

Rivalry of souls.

Counterposed. Overcommunicating. Destigmatizing. Patholology. Overbarriering.

My world for itself and my world for me.

Constagnation.

·✛·

The choking feeling of absolutely needing to be in a hopping motion. A tamed dancing bear in the circus. A minion cleanforming of the space delineated already by the first of two feet of superiorised two-leggedness, and the still obsessive intent to enter anyone's backyard through a window. St. Vitus's rock-n-roll dance and desire for a blinking of an eye which obligingly respects certain unwritten directions. The desperate movement on the same spot, seemingly parodying (but only seemingly) a continued movement away from the spot, that unsatiable disquieting swinging back-and-forth of a God, indeterminate through an internally tense, intensified, non-unique and vascillating one.

·✛·

From the inside out, but from which inside to which outside?

Imagine all that we could without the little word "if", thus unconditionally. All that we could (could we?) only just then, if it were unconditional. Thus without the right to choose, so we couldn't.

And then it becomes a word, when reality is reforged through the act of writing into . . .

The accordion of life.

Inexgratiating.

She looks at you, and depending on what she sees from the outside, she locates that which lies within. Whatever truth may be, what we're talking about is truth through salvation. In looking into her eyes it becomes clear to me that a similar process of judgment is occurring within her as well. Since this concerns an unending process, the fact that such an encounter only lasts a fraction of a second is seen as a mitigating circumstance.

Bearing the witness to that which is not yet complete? But there is no other alternative.

·✦·

Appearance lies, because it is lied to.

A heart, which frozen . . . endures?

Golemology.

The word "outsider", and its semantic uncleanliness.

Shorttermness; longtermness.

Seeking only the impossible within impossibility.

Unresistance.

The invisible prosthesis of the Internal becomes transformed in the shape of an external shape.

Apotheosis of innocence?

Nothing beautiful in anything beautiful.

At each point of finality, and at the ultimate point.

Schizophrentic.

The need to ignite at every fire that's burning. To ignite oneself, but not burn out.

Inclined to be abused.

Leading incapabilities.

Egocenter.

That will surely have a reason, we think to ourselves and, precisely because of this, we devalue it.

Categorical categorization.

Preversion.

For that from which he suffers is increasingly readable in his countenance.

Bookish learners and scholarly goals.

Enchantment.

From objectivity to precision.

Everything into the depths of everything.

Interproductive.

Childhood dreams of childhood and childhood dreams of maturity.

Unquestioned by unambiguity.

Defacto.

Making visible the visible and hiding the invisible.

Excessive sorrow.

Presupportive.

Before that which is unreal unto that which is real, yet elude we must.

To find something that is not nothing.

Bottom whole.

And battling with a high point against the adjacent?

The dissatisfaction of satisfaction.

Excoded.

Musicians, who go deaf over time and therefore preventively remove especially powerful loudspeakers from their houses, replacing them with smaller and smaller speakers that expressly spare their hearing—and not only this. There are music critics who, simply for health reasons, at a certain point in their career dispose of their rich collection of music, accumulated over time, that suddenly has no more meaning for them. Then we have St. Thomas Aquinas who, with great foresight in his late, yet still productive age, made the lucid revelation that his lifelong efforts in the guise of his life's works were worth—

Counterfaking

He: A living question mark, a question mark so full of life as a question can be. The question of one who could draw no breath, the question with each suppressed tendency to breathe out. The question to an answer which yields no answer to a question. The question to a question that doesn't answer, even when it does.

Being asked what he was doing, he answered that he had no time.

Spontaneous obligation.

For everything he is grasping for (as a drowning man) constitutes a breakthrough in his life.

Prior to that which was, and after that which shall be.

Empathology.

Non-communicability of pain, which is only effective when connived.

Every experience remains somewhat indebted to me.

Endlessification.

His respect of the power that never knew how to differentiate the power from bravado.

Searching and feeling around.

Decreation.

In the emotional bandwidth of emotion.

Time assembled.

What do internal feelings do before they are internalized (and how, actually) and who says they necessarily have to do something?

Cataclysman.

And relate to oneself (to one's life) polemically.

Not able to be thought through, or not able to be thought away?

Violating.

A long term, eternal diagnostic of the condition (or of the relationship) as an everlasting pronunciation of that which is unspoken.

Idioms of duration?

(T)autology.

In searching for the infinity by searching within infinity.

Two alike, always equally.

The limits of friendship, delineated by the friendship and the limits of love, dreadfully circumscribed by nothing at all.

Ergonautics.

Nothing in which believing means . . .

The thundering of chocalatey nights.

One related to the other and one related to themselves, thus to anyone.

Complete utilization.

A heart perfect.

"Is this still the way?" asked the wayfarer.

Romantic ideas refined by reality into romantic ideas refined by reality.

Undefying.

Extremism of every extreme that perceives it as such.

Halving God's help using the Devil?

The how-much-ness of the fall.

Transformat.

The mastery of the need of the mastery of the need of the mastery of the need . . .

Unto the wretchedness of defiance (of rebellion).

Into the thick of that which aims.

Undefamation.

The need to improve one's better Self, within the need of the worse Self to embrace such a need.

Preleaps and prefalls.

Anachromatic.

Refrain from violence to achieve imperviousness? But how?

A thought harmed by deeds and a thought harming the deed.

Unexfermenting.

On the rock bottom of that which, at least, has a bottom.

The fetish of language.

Unmisunderstandable.

A deadly rare illness.

The truth of the chess player and the truth of the chess piece.

Masking to the core.

Centripetal path.

The filling of space, and its emptying.

Uncalmability.

A few sentences in friendship, the indication of an understanding, like a condom.

A certificate of pain.

Dosing out.

Paying attention to that which is being observed. "An XY, the singer of XY group, killed his lover in a moment of insanity, the actress XY, whose husband XY commented on the event as follows . . ."

Against all forms of lying. Against all forms of truth.

Uninfallibility-making.

For how can we dictate the good, what should it be and what should it not?

Sensory flavours.

Enanchoring.

And now we take the step up to overstepping . . .

Disaspiration and deinspiration.

Exunwinding.

A humorless show-off is unimagineable.

Not to see reality in oneself reflects the need to be real.

Unsentenced for life.

The absolutorium of the absolute.

Constructed humanity and inborn humanity.

Catcheting.

And the organism of any act (does every act have its organs?)

Forms of flightiness.

Hindwhispering.

Is infinity the antithesis of finitude?

All-too-much life.

Unshifts.

When needing to share, do we need to share stability, progress, or stagnation?

Neurotic wings.

Decalculation.

So many words, so many languages.

Value-added story.

Unsurmountedness.

Complete isolation from the reality that is completely cut-off from reality.

The luxury of emotional tension?

Impositions.

An element of the whole that will suffocate every detail at its very core.

With the hand, cast before the glove.

Unjailed.

When can it still be said that some of the thrown boomerangs will come back; and when do the boomerangs just keep coming back?

Years later, drop by drop.

Experi*mentor*.

And every conflict, always in favor of a final result, and vice versa.

A painful life or a life pain?

Opening ad infinitum.

Tongues, captured behind the teeth.

Exhausted needs and needs which need yet to be exhausted.

Unobliged.

Conscience feeling or guilty feeling?

Visions of the blind.

Poisonweight.

To strive for life means to materialize life, to metamorphize life into material (for what experiment, who knows).

To survive — by default?

Deincarnate.

The ideal is that which is ideal about what is certainly far from ideal.

On a map there is no loop angle.

Anti-coma.

In dire need you shall find a friend in dire need.

Disconcerting ornaments.

Ingradation.

Yes. It's certainly better not to know some truths, but how then can authenticity of those things be guaranteed that differ from them?

✛

Be it as it may, it appears as if she was just performing it all out before you. As if obliged to be shut off from anything without, she expands her innermost outwards to all sides as if dealing with something tangible. Without consideration of the obstructions placed in her way, or on the contrary with consideration of it, and therefore precisely inconsiderate. Through an internal spiraling drain she sucks, from the outside, anything that seems worth bothering with. And she instinctively pushes everything else, whatever that may be, with the same iron will and diligence, away from herself. And you pose like a passerby who claims no ownership right to any of this. Like someone that shouts out their visions to the distraught territory of possibilities of which each is, at any given moment, ready to negate the other visions in an all-too-wide gesture of a form's self-destruction, a form which has barely had the opportunity to finish shaping itself.

The fear of putting something in her hand (ungraspable devouring?) and suffering through it with her. Sensing the unbearable tension the consequence of which is imbalance.

Where does the run-up end so that it can still be stopped? Or is it better to avoid this and try the whole thing anew, in a different way? But how? How should we consummate our longing without permanently diminishing it, and to what end?

Observing people from a bird's-eye view, unto which one must succumb. He's this and she's that, look! But who is he and who is she? Is it important? For whatever is natural can serve the unnatural as a model. But can the unnatural, if it looks naturalness in the eye (which is formulated as a moral imperative), see something other than, of all things, its unnaturalness…? Always leaning against something which exists not, until it reaches the yearned-for dimension of falling that defies the fall. Always focused to the point of unfocus, the mystical glance of the eyes or whatever one cares to call it. While only expecting that which cannot not arrive, but since always, and expecting … Assuming that this could be rejected through action, and go on rejecting it through an action you will, and despite. Do it all over from the beginning, doing it again and again and again. Retouch it. Initially you have to completely retouch it, and then comes the counter-retouching. A young man in his middle years comes to understand this who, over the course of time, comes ever closer and more precisely to settle down in a place that is only familiar to him. And since only in the folds of one's soul decimating faults appear, it's good to know what needs to be patched together.

Retrograding.

Concealed contents which dart about the text aflame. Yes, aflame. But one can't test, however, *what* sets them on fire — one would burn one's fingers in the process.

⁘

As the embodiment of a suicide you glide through life, using solely those streets behind whose corners salvation lurks. For you know that that which is waiting for you behind them in these moments reveals itself to that other within you at another moment on the right side of expectations. On the side from behind which this expectation drives your imagination onward using an awkward non-powered engine of a desperate urge for that which lurks around the corner. Hence your path becomes shorter and shorter without these corners. The path measured with the imaginary No of every expectation is a path which whispers this No above all else. Saying Yes to No makes this path a certainty that you heartbreakingly choose to follow. On a repeatedly doctored photo of the past towers into the future a wick which, hopefully, no one will light.

A pact of rebellion.

·✢·

Mystery as a component of the inexplicable, a mode of existence, and mystery as a part of the unexplained, a game mode.

Monodimensionality of death, always one of its dimensions.

The emptying of the empty.

Perifairy.

⁘

Having strayed from one past, one is waiting for the next.

Unsolvable, or unresolveable?

Playing with fire threatens the fire.

He dies as if he lived.

Sadistic facts.

⁘

That one who constantly asks whether or not they have a right to exist is just as unbearable as they who doesn't feel this need at all.

For people who mutated to counselors (a miracle that they didn't become scientists!) are instinctively digressing, and their instincts know very well why. And they know this even without having known something or other, for *what* can instincts know at all? And science? It scientifies, therefore neither does science, actually, know in the truest sense of the word. Science, which metamorphoses a purely unscientific object — its object of research (with the intention of scientifying it?) — into a scientific object.

Deathly ill? No, vitally ill.

De-interpretation.

Fatal decision-making. (There are no fatal decisions, for *every* decision is fatal).

The flightiness of thoughts and the flightiness of acts.

And with every discretion, a necessary element of inspection.

A Dream, January 12, 2006

It occurred somewhere in Slovakia at a time that today is irretrievably gone, that however endures deep within me, in the guise of deeply rooted archetypes. One of these archetypes is a typically slimy Slovakian bar of the lowest grade, resident (its archetype, that is) in my imagination, I know not why, and always invokes an exceptionally lyric ambiance about it. In one of these bars, on the basis of vague recollections of a real place that I sought out on the way home from school (the bar being about halfway along the way), I happened to find myself in it, I guess either brought along or planted there, most probably by my father's friend. I see there — is it him really? — a top-notch writer, who just loves coming to such low-class bars, and surely because he never had any money. He was an excellent writer whose recent books, however, had receded somewhat in terms of quality. Perhaps he had only put them together for publication just to get the advance, who knows. This writer had always been, as far as I know, a great admirer of Dostoyevsky, just as my father who asked me quite recently to return some of the Dostoyevsky volumes that I had long moved to my place, leaving him only the dustjackets. To be quite honest, this writer *himself* seemed a little bit like Dostoyevsky to me, perhaps more from appearance, his way of laughing (for I assume that Dostoyevsky was different from Rilke or Bataille and could even laugh spontaneously sometimes), I don't know what exactly, but they were things concerning his personality itself rather than those things we might find in his books. It had been a long time since we had seen each other, but I know that my father had been present then, too, even bothering to make an observation that could have hurt the writer (something along the lines of "the art of growing old", in the context, if indirectly brushed upon, of reflecting on the image of the writer as a *man massacred by life)*. Briefly, my father had the feeling that he appeared better and expressed it, though in so doing had already forgotten that he not only looked better but was also more successful, well-off and so on, which he even drove to the extreme when he suddenly began speaking about his experiences with women (and this too in a way where he wasn't speaking about himself, but about Casanova, which at that point in time was fully irrelevant, since it sounded far from convincing). The aforementioned encounter which I'm referring to here played out in the rooms of an institution with a de facto political purpose, which however didn't prevent people in any way from simply meeting there (just for a chat) and even having a drink, like in a bar. It was an *intimate political*

space, in its way, a rendezvous space for the post-revolution-
ary elite, serviced by amiable and charismatic female crea-
tures whose presence contributed to the secrecy and almost
hominess of this club. Yet now we found ourselves in another "institution" which in fact was the previously mentioned
low-class bar, and I'm sitting next to the writer (father isn't
there), and he gracefully acknowledges my presence and par-
dons me — my father's improprieties as well as my own — I
can see it in his eyes. And I am grateful to him for it. Suddenly, however, he's gone again and I find myself in a house
of pleasure. All the intimate scenes unfolding there occur in
a large salon which, although being on a few levels and dark-
ened or illuminated by precisely arranged light installations
from different angles, is one space nonetheless, in fact the
only one at that. As to the particulars that I "experienced"
in this place, I can't recall much, I only know that my need
that I sought to nurse here remained unfulfilled. This was
also at least partially because I suddenly caught sight during the *seance* of a woman who was coming towards me in
big strides, hence unstoppably — and right on past to the
checkout and then to the coatroom —, a fully-grown woman, with strict black bangs, much in the guise of Lulu from
the well-known film *Pandora's Box*. This was my father's col-
league from whom I had to hide rather quickly as it suddenly came to my mind that she was only here to check if I was
hanging out here by coincidence. Quickly I slid into the tub
standing next to me so as not to be seen. From the side I was
able to observe how she chattered with the coatroom lady,
from whom she had already obtained the number to my

locker, for — and only now this is quite clear to me — Father
had left the key to the hotel room in my pocket.

·✦·

They want milk but despise the cow. They want art but despise artists.

Mythology, or mythologic?

Spreading wings.

And a flame that stretches forth its tongues from any sort
of friction.

Airy gasses.

Contra-evolution.

And whatever we may take seriously, whose structure being
ripped apart . . .

And so that words do not function like scenery.

Chronotypes.

The revolution that consumes its goals.

Layering of pain.

Represervation.

Sweet children from good families for sweet children from good families.

What does death do? It deathens.

Wonderguilt.

Unintentional and barely inherent timing of will which causes the everlasting scream and cackling.

For I don't know what to do with what I do not know.

Intimitation.

The uniqueness of death—always the first of its consequences.

Contra-acting and contra-facting.

Singlicity.

And when reality stops being a possibility, falling for a possibility, as if it was reality.

Expressing the core in our outness?

Enrealizing.

The objectivization of the objective, as if we were dealing with something subjective.

The aggressiveness of the activity and the activity of aggressiveness.

Decapitulation.

And they're constantly waiting for new truths, generally designated as *material*.

A Dream, January 24, 2006

I find myself in a city in which a catastrophe occurs. I'm visiting people in different apartments, the common denominator is a certain kind of exclusivity, although in most of the cases we're not talking about the highest class apartments. I especially notice their furnishings. They're all very cosy yet at the same time have a bit of a bunkerish feeling to them. Two, in particular, I remember well. The one was located in a tower which we had to climb a spiral staircase to reach, finally ascending to the top and being informed that we were at the top of Big Ben. I recall quite well the incredible view from up there, as well as my exclamation: God, what a view! And the other apartment that lingered in my memory was located on the opposite pole ... but of what? We were situated on a luxury terrasse at a quasi-party, when suddenly, only a few meters away from us, a bus stopped and workers with filthy faces and equipment disembarked, darting a flighty look at us before moving on. I believe that the surprise, even the latent horror of this encounter was greater on our side than theirs (even if a certain degree of surprise could be detected in their countenances). Between these two apartment visits occurred merely a kicking about through the streets, meaning nothing, just a pointless accumulation of material, for the characteristic mark of the people moving on these streets was just the mere fact of their permanent motion. Each of them was heading to a particular place and only unwillingly would or wouldn't permit us to know as witnesses of this mish-mash.

What could be more absurd than self-destruction as a protest against destruction? (Aren't the true reasons behind masochism rooted in this idea?)

An exchange of words with my father. "Help yourself, then others will be helping you." I repeat my favorite Nietzsche quote in the usual context of my will to act, which presses on for self-affirmation. Father echos the saying in a slightly altered version: "Help yourself, then God will help you." And this caused me to think of Kierkegaard.

Multiplying even without faith in that "aggregating from ourselves?"

Sublimited lust for life.

Literary circles. One for whom the point is not to kill themselves, and the other who can entertain themselves with it.

Archetypal imperative?

My tracks—and the tracks that track me down.

Monophrasability

And climbing, one against the other, the steps of the escala-
tor so that this time it is he who victoriously steps out first
from the rolling track of the purgatory subway towards you,
about to enter its insides (so that you're the one, though,
that sinks down, beaten, and he the one that rises). In the
fraction of a second you catch sight of one another, and the
transfer, one to the other, a moment's snapshot of yourself.
Dress up elegantly so that no peering eye can gain any in-
sight into the patchwork of the soul. Put on the hat and a
blank expression, that suppressed sorrow of a suppressed joy.
   And in the whole city pictures are hanging in cafes that
display pages of the author's diary showing where they had
led him that the author took and recorded as entries of a diary where *these* recorded him. On every picture at a singular
given moment, which as the only one from him succeeded
in being—as in "existing"—beyond the framework of the
author's complete diagnosis. It seems to me that in the spite
of this person not only a superficial revolution is represent-
ed, but rather the attitude of someone fallen who under-

stood with bitter pride how to raise his situation to the level of the pathway.

The ego during a process (I cannot, do not know, do not want to . . .) and ego as that through which the Ego from the Non-Ego is differentiated.

Cacommodation.

·⊹·

Completeness doesn't give a damn about the search for completeness, and therefore the 'positive' of the Christian God consists of the fact that he does give a damn.

Between loneliness and estrangement.

A broad understanding of the human being.

Magic, summoned through magic rituals, drawn from summoned rituals.

And dogs barked, and children clung to impatient mothers.

A value symbol.

The exception presupposed by a rule (the essence of that exception) assumes an exception presupposed by another rule (the existence of that exception).

Stray spirit and stray soul.

An act of inactivity.

⊹

And yet another of my 'friends' slithering through this town, foaming at the mouth. Whenever I meet him I lose bucks on his account. All the while he banters about singularly lofty things. He's always in the middle of things, so it seems, and even has someone who takes care of his suits. And the course of the world—however it was created—is precisely tuned to the running of the film in his head.

For everyone that is not healthy needs a doctor. And accordingly, since *each one* needs *their own* ...

⊹

They hang an end (from their perspective) around your neck like a leash and set you as a negative law of a "not-like-this-anymore". From time to time they shunt the coordinates and with it the locations (where this all takes place) as well—those traps for the trusting little animals. Those animals whose despairingly aggressive yelping, meowing or grunting immediately invokes the spiteful attention of a device that sets out pell-mell hacking off hands, feet and heads.
    And whereupon you wander through the city as if your head's gone, hashed-smashed to pieces by their devilish de-

mand to devour you while still alive, as an appetizer.

Prediction and reprediction.

The barely noticeable tenseness of a facial expression—
which, after all, can also be faked (he's not evil, take note,
he's solely considering things)—which makes it possible
without even any sort of internal remonstrations to define
someone as a person who isn't searching with one's glances,
but—watch out—*is lurking*.

(And these are the entanglements that concern man wherever he pops up, wherever that may be).

The starry sky above me—my castle.

That it would please them.

That they would perform magic tri-i-icks with their intimacy, skin stripped off.

And with their selfsame intimacy, stripped of all intimacy, that they would rip open their wounds in a public display.

And learning new things in order to be able through them

to refute the old things (and all this while they still exist).

Someone and Noone — and noone between.

In my language with my tongue.

And respecting someone on the basis of one's own criteria — on the basis of criteria by which in respecting others we respect ourselves.

Intermittentthrough.

The ideal as the norm?

The decay of mores and moral decay.

For *every* nation is degenerated. (The nation is an idea that degenerated).

Preliminaring.

That which keeps me alive and that which keeps me from being (the important part is that it keeps me).

As if the traps — intentionally — had something in mind for us.

That which is playing out here, and that which is being played out.

Insufficiently mad?

To experience something exceptional and, thus, to deny the exceptionality of that which is not.

Cognital.

⊹

And the glowing longing in her eyes, invoking all this. Constantly measured, pale, with an almost unnaturally soft skin, which she strokes sensually with her fingertips. And it's precisely this that keeps her in that meditative apathy which she always interrupts unexpectedly with something, if something induces her to *exude her laugh from deep in her throat* that she's suppressed until that very moment. A laugh, unleashing her spite like a drop from a precipice. At that moment her eyes disappear. Something in the depths of her laugh is so enthralling that it causes goosebumps.

Today she's departing to China. Probably something stirred in her to turn a new leaf to finally learn something. She no longer wants to help herself like a parasite to all those things she unconsciously attracts. She said: "My parents humped like rabbits, while they hated each other." There was no merriness in that statement.

Nothing that would have been worth a catharsis through a crime.

A Dream, February 21, 2006

It's dark and gradually all the lights are going out. Her arrival has been well anticipated beforehand. Thus the "gradually", which in fact means the transition from electric lighting to the flickering dancing flames of burning candles. Everything unfolds slowly, ritually silent. At the same time I observe how everyone is working. I see my publisher, but also two young editors of the erstwhile *Prague Literary Review*. I think Markéta is there as well, the reserved fifth editor of the magazine who's moving quite animated & sleekly through the living room and in so doing reminds one of the motion of the fire whose main purpose—besides producing light— consists of propagating shadows and other playful images in the room, casting them all over. Yet somehow everything is quite gloomy. I open the bathroom door right next to the kids' room (that I had to leave in order to pee in peace) and I determine that there's no light here, either. And so I leave the door a bit ajar with a slight sense of foreboding. I also perceive my father's presence—and as it is *his* household, this is by no means unnatural, what's unnatural is rather what on earth *the others* are doing there. Can it be that it all has to do with a sort of conspiracy? I catch sight of a newspaper lying strewn on the floor. What's that? *Samizdat*? Is this whisper that's coming from the distant living room the noise of conversing people (or solely their shadows)?

Fascinography

Killing the pain within out of the necessity of its — hermetically sealed — invocations from the other side.

Prototruths and protolies.

Miracle-beautification.

And non-understanding in reward for non-understanding as a penalty.

Bared clauses.

And the problem of all that prostitution through which we allow ourselves . . . to get paid for bare being?

Deformulating.

⁘

And the story that goes on and on and thus gets more and more brutal. Not even the drapes change very much. Bars and discos and frozen lakes in the darkest night. Movement in all directions and constantly pristine, at least initially. And then there're the impossibilities of movement, the restrictions on the basis of dejection. And the laws of conservation of energy. And the impossibility of enduring, that endures. Opening arms wide — whatever possible things are ensnared in this embrace, so be it. The one a parasite and the other, able to be exploited by parasites. Thus it appears for those observers looking from the outside into the Internal. In the Internal, however, things are utterly different. In the Internal that in fact constantly looks outward but sees nothing, nothing but the fog which is part of its glance. That glance which is active, yet active not on the basis of an act, but rather a counter-act. For there is no absolute and all this which is not an absolute does not exist. And in spite of this, there's the effort to penetrate it, to enter into it. Not to fathom it any more, but solely bore through it with glances. For that which there is to see of life is solely the dead. It is *the* question, whether we are the ones killing it or if It is killing us. This has nothing to do with truth and love; this is a question of parallelism. To what degree can time be played out in alternative schemes? And what about space? Does it really only represent the curtains for the territories of our Internal? (And what's there in the Internal if, as we say, things are utterly different inside?)

PART THREE

Pointomania

These subliminal movements with which the moved moves the moving. That silent yet all the more effective sparking, invoked through it. These are neither coincidences and indeed, assuming we understand correctly, collisions. The conflict of singularity is only contestable for they who invoke this conflict. (Doesn't the origin of shivering fits on the basis of all this dwell in the a priori failure of resistance of the most internal? For what does the glance mean that hurriedly turns away from that which has not yet been, for this god forbid might be it?)

⋅⊹⋅

Indeed not, he says, at a loss, deflecting her flightily with his hands (the whore on the main road at about midnight). Quickly he wards her off with his No-instinct so that the counter instinct within him won't say yes. For them it's no longer to do with hard cash, let alone emotional desire. The whole point is to transsect a man's axis of movement. Invade that space and bring it into a state of vibration, till it threatens to burst.

Every executioner is their victim's kin.

Loops arise as we shun knots.

Cramping veins.

Good is good is good is good is good.

·❖·

And defusing the concept "Problem" of its moral tint? Yet what's left over then from such a mutilated problem?

Unbecoming.

Smearing one's own mouth through one's own name? But how else . . .

The glue of the aesthetic experience as a glue of an aesthetic of that which has been experienced.

Feeling-on-feeling.

The salve of hell?

The moral aspect of the mores and the mores of the moral aspect.

Neoformation.

·❖·

. . . and the shattered, that is one? But which?

. . . and so that the "I'm having a hard time" doesn't sound like a cliche.

. . . and embarassment of the pain.

. . . and the emptiness that one has to fill up so that it is no more.

. . . and the time that is against all eternity.

. . . and the misutility value (of men, of things, of thoughts).

. . . and the strategy of infallibility.

. . . and all that which for the bowed-to is not sufficient for straightening up.

. . . and the robbing of one's own (deincarnation?).

. . . and that yes means a Yes and no a No.

. . . and a contra-collision.

. . . and an openness which borders on the created.

⁘

And the mistakes of self-examination, the distancing of ourselves from them meant contradicting them completely; for what else is absolute questioning than fully exhausting contradiction. With all the emptiness of the strived-for strictness of the vague that, in so doing, wins nothing to its side. Behaving out in a certain manner. What is motive here, and what is attack? A colossal shock on the basis of misunderstanding, masked by colossal misunderstanding. As if the non-beginning through any beginning were to offer the confirmation of one, as if the latter could be random whatsoever. The things that don't even lose their validity by collision, the things whose loss of validity doesn't lead to collision. Wandering the streets with the work ethic of porn stars. Commemorating the contemplation, making it one's task. And if not, then she's there. That which violently twists and turns this way and that like a fish on the hook of an unknown fishhunter that lifts it high, somewhere or other, which the fish in the water can't see, though. Its consciousness is veiled behind an uncertain feeling of bliss — veiled nonetheless, since it cannot compare itself with anything at all. For the transversing of all necessary limits that hold us together, we lose the concept for the correct measure in a paradox harmony to the extent of our decay. Here, though, the point is not what an attentive spirit observes in or makes out from its contours. The point here is all about what's really happened, and if we were to see it as a history, that would mean we would concoct it entirely. Let's take a different approach, then. It looks like a ridiculous caricature. Of what, though, if it, under the close scrutiny of an opportunity, stands apart like a thorn (it, *the dove*) in an open wound? Under the scrutiny of an opportunity, that checks its possibilities and its irresistability. Under the scrutiny of an opportunity, under which all of its silences will turn nuts one day. To finally utter something. In the Autumn of 1993 I visited New York (in the event I don't count the brief summer episode in 1990) for the first time. Only some years later did I draw in my head the mindmap that at the very time and in the very place I was traipsing about, this (at that time still unknown to me) John Zorn had also been hanging about in the same places. A few years later when I was tracking his exploits in the underground, the connections that had intuitively led me to Zorn also led me to the connections to which his intuition had led him in the first place. In this respect I'm talking about a split, about the fact that we can split things apart endlessly if we want to. It's about the cunning search for the moment that can surprise us. Can insatiability be cunning? It is much the case as if you're looking for just the right moment to win approval under a girl's skirt. What's important is the search alone. The search as a gradual approach towards something, it being a kind of art in its own right, of suspending that approach. Best so that it would never occur and that the motion there would, at the same time, be a motion thence. And John Zorn, at least the way I understand it, is able to achieve this through his improvisations. To stay in the center, as if there was no beginning, always starting as if there were no end. The awareness of a perfect illusion, which is an awareness of perfection only so long as the illusion remains. An illusion, creating a space for its own fulfillment in the human brain. We are thus talking about filling the possible with the current, through what we call an act of intellect. And even this is only one aspect of the matter. As I returned to *my* New York after ten years, the first thing I needed to check was the presence—or lack of presence—of the few footholds which kept my head above water back when I stayed in the City. Not even counting the numerous side-impressions because, at the time, I did not frequent cultural establishments very much. For example, those giant underground chimneys and their billowy, creeping smoke, blown into space by a divergent wind. All this countered by Marián Varga's *Antiwar Requiem*, thundering into the headphones of my old walkman. Are we deepening a Shaft of Babylon? And on which floor does it start? Indeed, let's go back to that point where we've not yet begun, and where Orwell long since stopped. In a small Bagel Buffet where all the old-timers sat around (at least back then, at least for me) from somewhere in so-called Eastern Europe. They had met in the evenings in this same place for years. Their discussions were visually spacious, and to a certain extent it was some sort of a map unfolding get-together. This used to be here, that—there. And then such and such happened. While at this subject I can't get around mentioning her soft lips—similar to a fishmouth—in my eyes, the exact opposite of a strong will, which is exemplified in hard-headedness and doggedness. And no, I'm not saying that soft lips don't know how to suck in and in so doing make a noticeable grimace. I'm not saying that at all. At the world premiere of Zorn's *Necronomicon* quartet composition, we both grimaced, deadly serious and, in so doing, we made extra sure not to look at each other, either. It was wonderful.

⸶

There is no solution. It is *the* solution.

An excess excised from another?

Overrevealing.

The hope that only dies when it has died.

And his indivisible division.

Contrarhetorics.

The *technology* of everything bad and the good that cannot be taught.

Principle of renewal?

Half-emptiness.

And meting out the limits of snares (for what else is a snare, if not a limit?).

Patent on light and patent on darkness.

Monoanimous vote.

And getting rid of oneself, as if one could be rid of something that one's merely borrowed.

Manouevring between footholds.

Expaining.

And reopening a wound (the blossom) so that it doesn't dry out.

Longing as a calling?

Wingbreakers.

And life, which we may proliferate with impunity, unlike everything that is subordinate to falsification (in other words everything else).

Protolocks and protokeys.

Humania.

And no single image of this world—however complete and comprehensive it may be—will ever reproduce the Original.

Everything that has a history and a history of everything.

Overcloning.

Entering life with a certificate of exceptionality?

Shadow execution.

Unthinking.

My thanks to Miluš Kotišová for
reading through the translation.
—Author

RÓBERT GÁL was born in 1968 in Bratislava, Slovakia, and, after a period of study and itinerancy in New York and Jerusalem, currently resides in Prague. He is the author of several books of aphorisms and philosophical fragments, one of which, *Signs & Symptoms*, is also available in English translation.